Our
Love
Grows

For my cousins Claudio, Rebecca, and Linda…
remember the pandas! And for Big Uncle and Izzy.

Published by Sourcebooks Jabberwocky, an imprint of Sourcebooks, Inc.
P.O. Box 4410, Naperville, Illinois 60567-4410
(630) 961-3900
Fax: (630) 961-2168
www.sourcebooks.com

Library of Congress Cataloging-in-Publication data is on file with the publisher.

Source of Production: Leo Paper, Heshan City, Guangdong Province, China
Date of Production: January 2016
Run Number: 5005297

Printed and bound in China.
LEO 10 9 8 7 6 5 4 3 2 1

Our Love Grows

ANNA PIGNATARO

sourcebooks
jabberwocky

In the deep green forest, Pip asked, "Mama, when will I be big?"

"You're bigger than you were before," said Mama.

"Once,
this tree
was smaller too.

And the stars above were just a few...

Your paw print was tiny in the snow,
and every step was far to go.

Birdy was all bright and new

and Blankie covered all of you.

Our favorite song went on and on.

Hide-and-seek took oh-so long.

Flowers bloomed and petals fell.

Pinecones tumbled down as well.

Tiny, you fit in my arms,
your little face, snug in my palms.

Like all these things and just like you...

...my love for you has grown bigger too."